PRIMAL

JESSICA GADZIALA

1

Maribelle

How many times had my grandmother told me that I should never be alone in the woods at night?

It had to be about a thousand times. Along with the advice that if you were alone and heard your name called, never to answer it. And that if you are taking a hike and feel like you are being watched, to never look behind you.

I always thought she was, you know, a cooky old broad full of Appalachian folklore.

My summers were full of her little snippets of seemingly silly advice amongst snapping green beans and baking pies.

Even a couple decades later, I still found snapping green beans on the front porch—or in my case in the city, on my balcony—oddly therapeutic. And nothing boosted my mood like a good session of procrasti-baking, having my tiny apartment full of the sweet scents of berries and the rich tang of butter.

There were so many times in my life that I longed for her tiny cabin at the feet of the Appalachian mountains, the slow pace of the long summers I spent with her, the detachment from the craziness of the world.

Hell, that was the very reason I'd left my life behind with only a few boxes of my belongings in the backseat of my ancient car, and made the long drive from New York to Virginia.

To rest.

To recover.

To figure out what the hell I wanted to do with the rest of my life.

My grandmother had passed a few seasons before, leaving her little cabin to me "for when you need to plant those roots somewhere."

I'd been too heartbroken to show up before.

And the first thing I did when I stepped on the creaky floorboards of the front porch was well up and sob for the better part of the afternoon.

It took a solid week to be able to get the place cleaned of cobwebs and critters who'd found little nooks and crannies to creep in.

It wasn't until all that cleaning was done, and I felt comfortable in the cabin, that I started to venture out.

There was the overgrown garden, full of weeds and volunteer plants that kept growing, dropping their fruits and therefore seeds, and regrowing year after year, even without any assistance.

If I were still around for the next year, I would be eating an abundance of tomatoes, greens, and squashes.

As it was, though, fall was steadily approaching, so all there was to eat were a few overly ripe tomatoes and pumpkins that had vined everywhere.

Leaning down, I tightened my shoelaces before making my way toward the mountains, seeking the silence, the peace inside my mind that I knew as a little girl exploring their mysterious depths.

Back then, my grandmother had taken time to tack little red ribbons to the trees that would lead me well into the woods, but lead me right back to the house.

Follow the ribbons and you will always be safe, Mari.

There were brave moments when I was young and reckless where I would venture off the path, but only a couple dozen yards, always keeping the ribbons in sight.

But it had been many summers since I'd visited my grandmother. Getting older, I'd wanted to spend my time exploring the city with friends than in the woods with the bugs and the snakes and all the crap I thought I'd somehow "grown out of."

So I was on my own as I walked, though there was still a clear path that led up toward the mountains.

The problem was, by the time I'd realized that I couldn't even see the cabin anymore when I looked back, it was already starting to get dark.

Panic, raw and familiar, gripped my system. It was the sweat that started to break out across my skin, the sick feeling in my belly, the hypersensitive hearing that I developed.

I knew, logically, that the predators of the Appalachias had been on decline for decades. That didn't mean, though, that there were no bears, bobcats, or coyotes still hanging around.

Oddly enough, though, it wasn't those things that I felt the most panic coming forward at that moment.

No.

All that I could focus on was my grandmother's words.

About things that went bump in the night, that were capable of saying your name.

"You're being ridiculous," I assured myself as I reached up to tighten the elastic around my long blonde hair that suddenly felt like it was too visible under the bright moon.

Was it full?

Nothing good happens under a full moon in the woods, Mari.

I was letting my mind run away with me.

I just needed to take a couple deep, calming breaths, and try to retrace my steps.

Even in the dark, the "path" was still somewhat visible.

I just needed to get on it, stay on it, and make my way home.

It was right about then, as I was giving myself a little pep talk, that I heard a distinct crunch behind me.

And not the little rustling of the underbrush or the sound of a little paw stepping on a twig.

Oh, no.

That was a big paw.

I knew the rule.

You never, ever, ran from a predator.

You never, ever, wanted to engage their primal drive.

You didn't want to become prey.

But in that moment, it wasn't my Appalachian summers brain that kicked in, it was my every-other-day city brain. Where the predators were of the two-footed variety, and running was often the only way to escape getting mauled.

So I didn't look back.

I didn't think twice.

I just bolted.

See, now, the whole purpose of starting to take daily hikes was because, well, the last year of a shitty job in an increasingly unfulfilling city had led to a bit of a, well, depression. And that depression mixed with the all-too-convenient food delivery services where I didn't even have to open the door and talk to anyone? Yeah, it meant I'd packed on some pounds.

Almost fifty of them, to be exact.

So I'd promised myself that I would get my body active again, and maybe drop a few of them while I figured out what my future held for me.

The thing is, those extra pounds and the past year of being completely sedentary, yeah, it slowed me down a lot more than I could have anticipated.

I mean, I wasn't expecting to have to, you know, run for my life. Had I known that was going to be a part of my reality, maybe I would have started cardio a little sooner.

It was a little too late now, though, as I tore through the woods, completely losing track of the path in a matter of minutes. And the lack of a path meant I was running face-first into branches that whipped my face until I had the mind enough to raise my arms and cut those up instead.

My lungs burned. Each ragged breath felt like swallowing fire.

But with each stride, I could hear the feet behind me.

Following me.

With the small bit of oxygen able to help my brain think straight, I thought that it was weird that whatever it was that was behind me was following at exactly my pace.

That was weird, right?

I mean, I felt like I was slowing down with each passing moment.

Which meant that it should have been able to overtake me.

Right?

If it was capable, why wasn't it?

What kind of predator toyed with its prey first?

Cats?

Big cats?

I didn't remember my grandmother warning me about the kinds of cats that could take down a full-grown woman, though.

Fear, prickly and electric, sparked through my system, distracting me enough that I missed it.

The downed tree right in front of me.

I didn't know it was there until it was too late, until I was falling forward over it, until I was flying through the air for one heart-dropping moment, before slamming down on my palms.

The rocks and twigs and underbrush bit at my skin, ripping it open, letting the dirt in.

Which should have been the least of my concerns, but I couldn't seem to stop my mind from panicking about possible infections.

I knew what I was supposed to do.

If you were down and there was nothing around to defend yourself with, you had one choice.

Curl into a ball and use your hands to protect your throat and neck. Then hope they got sick of mauling and eating you before they hit any vital organs.

Did I do that, though?

No.

No, of course not.

Because, clearly, something was wrong with my brain right then as I threw myself onto my back, intent on facing down whatever was following me.

And there it was.

The biggest freaking wolf I'd ever seen in my life.

I mean, no, I hadn't exactly seen a lot of wolves in person. Or, you know, any wolves. But I was pretty sure they weren't supposed to be so big.

Clearly, he was eating well.

Feasting on stupid human flesh who didn't know better than to get stuck in the woods after the sun set.

I was scrambling backward before I was even aware of telling my brain to do so as those yellow-brown eyes pinned me, watching me, likely trying to figure out how many bites it would take to consume me completely.

I barely scuttled back two feet before it was arching backward, then leaping over the downed tree, flying right at me.

The scream that came out of me was ear-piercing, coming from somewhere buried deep as I watched its gray furry belly coming over me.

I slammed backward, my head knocking off the ground hard.

And that was the reason, surely it was, that I saw what I thought I saw.

A man bursting from the beast.

But I couldn't convince myself of that a second later as the body came over mine, pinning it to the ground.

The muscled, naked body.

I was having a stroke.

Did people hallucinate with a stroke?

I was pretty sure they didn't.

A psychotic break? Maybe.

Or did I inhale some psychedelic mushroom spores?

Something was clearly very wrong with me, though. Because I was not only seeing a naked man, but feeling him on me.

My breasts, heaving with all the running, were pinned to his wide, strong chest.

My hips were under his.

And, well, wasn't that his hardness pressed against my lower stomach?

It was time for that panic that I'd known a moment before. But it didn't seem to be building.

All I felt was a strange sort of disconnection and almost… peace.

Peace?

No.

No, that made no sense.

I couldn't be feeling calm with a strange, naked man on top of me with a raging hard-on while we were alone in the woods where there was no hope of anyone coming to save me.

Except I didn't really feel the need to be saved right then.

I felt almost, I don't know, drunk, or hypnotized or… I had no idea. I had no past reference for what I was feeling as I looked up into the face of a man who had just been a… wolf.

A big, scary, beautiful gray wolf with yellow-brown eyes.

But the man?

The man was somehow just as scary and beautiful with gray streaked through his dark hair and yellow in his brown eyes.

His face was chiseled with these impressive cheekbone hollows, a stern brow, a scar down his left cheek, and just the right amount of scruff.

"Mine," he growled before his head lowered, and his lips claimed mine.

And, well, I damn sure felt like I was his right then as his lips bruised into mine, as his teeth scraped my lower lip, as his tongue moved inside to toy with mine.

I should have been writhing and raking my hands over him and biting and kicking and trying to get him off of me.

All I did, though, was melt into the moment.

All I did was kiss him back.

And, sure, there was some writhing, but it was not the "get me out of here" sort. It was more of the "wow, this feels good, and I need more" sort.

When my fingers did eventually rake down his back, it wasn't to hurt him, but to find the muscles swell of his ass and sink my fingertips into it, holding him more tightly against me as my legs parted and let him slide between.

His cock felt thicker and longer pressed against the most intimate part of me. I couldn't seem to stop myself from grinding my hips up against him.

I needed that friction, that promise of relief to the clawing need building inside of me.

Needy.

God, I'd never been so needy before.

I felt like the intensity of the sensations could make me cry if they didn't get soothed, if they didn't find release.

"Mine," the man repeated as his lips broke from mine, leaving them swollen and overly sensitive as he headed toward my neck, his stubble scraping across my sensitive skin.

I was pretty okay with being his right then as his face dipped between my breasts, his tongue tracing a shape there as he lifted onto one arm so he could undo my buttons of my shirt, slowly exposing my chest and belly inch by inch.

His mouth followed the path his fingers cleared, his lips and tongue moving over my skin, down my belly, then back up and over, teasing over the edges where my breasts disappeared into my bra.

Then, his hand done with my buttons, it moved upward and yanked down one of my cups.

My nipple pebbled up at the brush of the cool air, making another of those growling noises escape the man on top of me before he was suddenly leaning down and sucking my nipple into his mouth.

My back arched up off the ground, pushing my breast against his sucking lips and stroking tongue as the need became a white-hot flame burning through my system.

His lips left me briefly, but only to go across my chest to continue the sweet torment.

My common sense never did return to me.

My hands grabbed the back of his head as he started to move downward again, his tongue tracing the waistband of my pants before he yanked against my hold and pushed back onto his heels.

His big hands moved out, grabbing one ankle so he could yank off one boot, then the other.

And what did I do?

I watched.

I watched this stranger in the woods who may or may not have been a, well, werewolf, strip me naked on the damn ground.

But the next thing I knew, his hands were grabbing the waistbands of my pants and panties, and dragging them down my legs.

He yanked up my legs once they were free, placing each of them on either of his shoulders, then leaning down and pressing a kiss to the inside of one of my ankles.

"Mine," he repeated again, but this time it was less of a growl, and more like a solemn oath.

I should have been analyzing that, along with the intensity in his gaze as he looked down at me, but the next thing I knew, he was kissing down the inside of my calf, my knee, my thigh, and any rational thoughts flew right out of my head.

My hips rose upward and my hands grabbed the back of his head as his tongue traced the crease of my thigh, needing him to move just a little bit more inward, to feel him tease over me, to put an end to the torment that had gripped my body.

There were three long beats as his face hovered, and I could have sworn I heard him whisper that word once again.

Mine.

But before I could decide, his tongue was tracing up my cleft, and everything else fell away.

My thighs started to shake as his lips closed around the bud of my clit, gently sucking it into his mouth over and over, somehow seeming to know exactly what I wanted. Like he was seeing into my mind and doing exactly what I was envisioning.

This was somehow cemented when all I could think of was the strange hollowness inside of me, the need for friction, for fullness, and then his fingers slid between and thrust inside of me, stroking soft and slow at first, then harder and faster as he drove me up.

His tongue replaced his lips, working me in unrelenting side-to-side movements as I writhed and arched and moaned for more.

He pushed me right up to that edge, leaving me hanging there for one agonizing second, before sending me free-falling off that cliff and down into an orgasm that seemed to start at the juncture of my thighs and spread outward until it overtook me completely.

My cries echoed out across the woods as the waves just kept crashing over and through me until they eased off, leaving me lifeless and panting on the forest floor.

Alone.

Alone?

That thought had me snapping out of my post-orgasm daze, looking around and realizing that there was no naked man over me or around me at all.

And there damn sure wasn't a freaking wolf there either.

"What the hell…" I hissed as I shot up to a seated position, my hands reaching for my clothes, covering up my near complete nudity.

Clutching my pants to my chest, my other hand rose, touching my head, wondering if I'd managed to hit it so hard that I'd… lost consciousness and concocted a wild dream.

That didn't explain my clothes being off, or the whole explosive orgasm thing. But, I don't know, maybe I was out of it enough to disrobe myself and reach between my thighs while dreaming about some hot wolf-man.

"Jesus," I hissed as I jumped up.

It didn't matter what had happened, really. What mattered was I had to get dressed and back to the damn cabin as soon as possible.

So that was what I did.

Shutting and locking every door and window then turning on every single light as I sat up in bed, realizing I should have listened to my grandmother.

Never be alone in the woods at night.

2

Waylon

"Way, where did you run off to?" Garrick asked as I made my way back toward our clubhouse in just a pair of pants I'd found hanging from a limb in the woods.

We tended to leave some clothing scattered around for the times when the Change came over us, and we didn't want to make our way back to the clubhouse stark fucking naked.

I mean, at this point, we were used to one another's naked bodies. That was just the way of things when we often ran together during a Change. But since some of the men were bringing women back to the clubhouse, it felt more respectful to cover at least the lower half before coming into the camp.

I'd grown up in these woods. We all had. Generations of shifters who recognized long ago that society wasn't a safe place for us.

The clubhouse was once a summer retreat for wealthy elites—a massive structure with over forty guest suites, outbuildings, and tennis courts surrounded by woods and its own private lake.

The pack was down to ten full-fledged wolves now, so we had more than enough room.

What we needed was, well, mates.

The True kind, not the fun one-night variety.

The kind who we could imprint on, claim, and build the next generation with. Build our numbers up. Return to our old glory.

So far, though, none of us had much luck.

Until, of course, last night.

We could Change anytime we wanted, but there was something powerful about the full moon, something that made it less of a choice, and more of a necessity.

It was when we were at our most base, our most primal selves.

That, perhaps, was why I smelled her from so far away.

The one.

My one.

My mate.

I had been around for so long, I didn't think I would ever find her.

Then, like a fucking miracle, there she was.

In the woods.

My woods.

Walking alone at night.

Beautiful.

So goddamn beautiful.

Her long blonde hair was pulled back in a steadily falling ponytail, soft little strawberry-vanilla scented tendrils falling down to frame her soft, heart-shaped face that was dominated by deep green eyes and plump pink lips.

And that body that was wrapped in a pair of cargo pants and a simple button-down—neither of which were meant for hiking, let alone at night—was thick and plump, the kind of body a man could sink his fingers into.

I didn't mean to get near her.

It was wrong.

Against the rules, even.

To fucking maul a woman in the woods in both wolf and human form.

It just hadn't felt like there'd been a choice. I had to get closer. I had to breathe her in. I had to feel her.

Something deep inside of me demanded it.

More.

Everything.

The next thing I knew, I was peeling off her clothes, filling my senses with her.

If I thought she was pretty clothed, she was fucking perfect bared to me, spread for me, fingernails digging into my skin, her breathing ragged, lips moaning for me.

Fuck.

My cock was getting hard again, even after taking care of the raging hard-on I'd walked away from her with hours before.

I had a distinct feeling that my cock was going to be at a near-constant state of aching desire until I surged inside her, until I felt her walls closing around me, her pussy squeezing my release out of me as she came.

"I, ah, got the scent of something," I admitted, not wanting to give anyone the whole truth yet, not until I was sure.

Sure that it wasn't just the moon, just the scent of a beautiful woman.

I had to know she was actually a True Mate before I told everyone else.

It would be a huge deal to the pack. No one had met a True Mate in our generation. Which was making everyone desperate to find one, to continue the pack's legacy, to create the next generation.

They would get nosy. Pushy. And would be extremely disappointed if I was wrong, and this random woman in the woods wasn't my fated mate.

It was best to keep it to myself until I could see her again. Not on a full moon. With my damn wits about me.

"Then I guess you don't need anything to eat," he said, waving over toward the massive pavilion where someone was grilling off some meat.

"I can always eat after being out all night," I said, shrugging, and following him toward the small crowd gathered around.

The entire day and night, all I could do was think about my mystery woman, about what it could mean if she was well and truly mine like every cell in my body was screaming out.

It was two full days before I could get away again.

And I went right back to the spot in the woods where I'd had her spread wide for me, her sweet taste flooding my mouth as she writhed under me.

To a normal man, they wouldn't have any trace of her left. To me, though, her scent was all around.

Taking deep breaths, I followed the scent of her back through the woods. She eventually made her way back to the path that had lead through the woods for as long as I'd been around, and I felt myself tensing as I followed them down the mountain, reasonably sure I knew where they were leading.

To a small cabin at the foot of the mountains.

The home of a legend.

And, in my pack, not the good kind.

As I got closer, and the scent got stronger, indicating it was a place the woman had been around for a while, leaving her intoxicating smell all around, I knew it.

The worst was, in fact, the case.

She was living in the cabin.

Which meant she was likely a descendant to the old woman who'd been there until her death a year or two before.

Greta Wilson.

A name that was damn near a curse in my pack.

My stomach twisted into a painful pit as I followed the tree line down the side of the house until I could see in the window in the front.

There she was.

A kick to the goddamn gut in all her casual beauty.

Her long blonde hair was down this time, swaying around her shoulders as she swept the living room floor.

She wore a simple tank top and shorts.

No bra.

Her perfect tits jiggled with each movement, making my cock stiffen as I thought about them in my hands, in my mouth, about my damn face buried between them, or my head resting on them.

Mine mine mine.

The animal inside of me was growling, damn near clawing at the ground, wanting to run, to pounce, to take her down, to make her well and fully mine once and for all.

But the history, the connection, that was what was holding me firmly in place.

The uncertainty.

The fear.

The potential for the past to repeat itself.

So I stood there.

And I watched.

With my cock aching in my pants.

Inside the house, she bent forward to sweep the dust into a pan, her top falling forward, giving me a great view of those swells of hers.

My hips involuntarily shifted, thinking of surging inside her, making my cock grind against the material of my pants, making a pained, frustrated groan escape me.

I watched as she turned, looking toward the trash can in the kitchen, then changing her mind, moving out the front door instead.

I stepped back into the tree line, disappearing to her, as she walked off the edge of the porch, and tossed the dust back to the earth, then stood there for a moment, looking out at the woods.

She placed the pan down on the railing of the porch and rolled her neck.

If the cabin had been abandoned since Greta's passing, the place had to have been a mess when this woman showed up.

Who was she?

A granddaughter, perhaps?

Why hadn't I ever seen her before?

Was she just one of those relatives who showed up after someone passed to clean up the mess, but never could be bothered to actually know the person while they were alive?

The beast inside me growled at the idea, not wanting to claim a woman who would be that heartless, that detached from their own history.

The rational side of my brain, though, had to put in its two cents about Greta, about what she'd done to us. So maybe this woman, potentially *my* woman, had her own sour history with the old lady.

Slowly, her arms rose, scrubbing at her cheeks for a second, then placing her hands over her eyes.

It took an almost embarrassingly long time for me to realize that she wasn't just rubbing her eyes.

She was crying.

Her body jolted with the sobs for a moment before she slowly lowered to her knees, her back hunched forward, huddling into herself as the sadness overtook her.

Mine, the wolf inside me whined, wanting to go to her, wanting to comfort her, to take the burden off her shoulders, make her smile again.

But I couldn't.

So I do all that I could; I stood there, silently supporting her from afar as she purged whatever ugliness she'd been holding inside of her.

It took a good, long time.

Eventually, though, she ran through it all, sitting back on her heels and wiping at her face for a long time before taking a breath so deep that her tits pressed hard against the material of her tank top, then exhaling hard and getting back up like nothing at all happened.

Before she went back into the cabin, though, her gaze slipped to the woods, scanning the tree line.

Then stopping with her gaze on me.

She couldn't see me.

But it was almost as if she… felt me there. Like maybe she sensed the connection as well.

She shook her head, like trying to talk some sense into herself, then going back inside.

What did I do?

Stood there for a long time before I realized that she'd gone into a room where I could no longer see her.

Frustrated, I carefully removed my clothes, leaving them on the spot, then letting the shift come over me, and running until I seemed to shake some of the confusing, mixed feelings inside of me.

I ran for hours, even washing off in the pond as the sun went down before I slowly made my way back toward my clothes.

Exhausted, distracted by slipping my clothes back on, I missed the sound of her approach.

But as soon as the shirt slid down my body and I could see again, there she was.

In a goddamned filmy white nightgown that I could practically see through, her soft hair falling around her shoulders, and her pretty face watching me.

"Who are you?"

3

Maribelle

I got back to the cabin and tried to do a search for the signs of some sort of traumatic brain injury before I remembered that my grandmother's cabin was stuck in the stone age.

There was no internet connection.

I could barely even make a phone call if I needed to.

I settled down with one of my grandmother's many reference books instead, poring over the pages, coming to the conclusion that it was entirely possible I'd sustained a hit hard enough to explain the hallucination or the dream if I'd lost consciousness.

I was choosing not to analyze why the hell I woke up naked and post-orgasm-contented.

No good could come from giving that whole situation too much thought.

There was one thing I *did* know, though. There was no such thing as freaking werewolves.

So I was probably just bleeding in my brain and would die a slow, lonely death over the next day or so.

Would anyone find my body?

I mean, eventually, someone would come looking for me, right? Sure, my parents were self-involved and had never given me too much thought in the past, so I couldn't imagine them wasting much of their time on me in the future. But they'd probably think something was a little odd when they didn't at least get a Christmas card from me.

Would I be nothing but bones when they found me?

Somehow, I found that more comforting than still being, you know, fleshy.

Why, might you be wondering, would I spend the day following a potential brain injury cleaning the cabin? Well, that would be because of my mother.

My neat freak mother.

It was always her voice in my head that peeled me off the couch on a Saturday after a hard week of work that left me feeling depleted and miserable, going to grab the cleaning supplies, and doing a deep clean of my entire apartment.

She certainly would have something to say about dying amongst all the filth in my grandmother's cabin.

So I cleaned it.

Then I showered.

Fed myself.

Wondered why I didn't feel like I was dying if I was.

Then I slipped into my prettiest nightgown that I'd bought after a long Jane Austen movie binge, finding those white nightgowns they wore so elegant and womanly and sexy in a subdued way.

And, yeah, I sat and, you know, waited for death.

That didn't seem too keen to come.

So I got up and paced restlessly, made and drank a cup of tea, then paced some more.

It was sometime after the sun set that I felt a strange pulling sensation, something that tugged so tightly that I felt helpless but to slip on my flip-flops and make my way out to the backyard, looking out over the darkness that almost made my eyes hurt it was so complete before I adjusted to it.

I thought, at first, that some part of me was just craving a little fresh air. But as I stood there, that strange pulling sensation was forcing me down the back path, going toward the mountains once again.

At night.

Like an idiot.

Even knowing that, though, couldn't seem to stop me or slow me down.

The strangest part was that something inside me knew where to go. I didn't feel like I was just randomly walking, not even when I stepped off the path and started walking in the woods kind of alongside the cabin.

In my mind, I flashed back to earlier that day, when I'd been having a little breakdown about my impending death before I even really got a chance to live much, and I'd felt an odd sort of vibration—for lack of a better term—coming to me from this part in the woods.

It had been both calming and soothing, exactly what I needed in that moment.

I'd shaken it off at the time, figuring it was just the whole "nature brings you peace and clarity" mindset that my grandmother always had.

But as I followed the strange tug inside of me, I was starting to wonder if there was something more to it.

Then there he was.

Kind of looking like Mr. Darcy coming out of the lake in that one Jane Austen adaptation, his hair dripping, his body glistening.

The same man from my so-called hallucination. The cause of my believing I had a brain bleed that would surely kill me soon.

The man who was a man, but also… not.

I wasn't even aware of my mouth deciding to say anything until the words were out of it.

"Who are you?"

I mean, it wasn't even what I really wanted to ask.

What are you was more like it.

But then those unique brown eyes with yellow flecks were pinning me, and I was finding it hard to form thoughts, let alone more words.

"Waylon," he said, and that voice was just as rough, just as gravelly and sexy as it had been when it growled out *Mine* over and over. "Way," he clarified.

"Way," I repeated, and I couldn't be sure, but it almost sounded like he kind of… rumbled at me when I said it. I mean, that was insane. I probably imagined it. "What are you doing on my property Way?" I asked.

Was it possible I'd crossed his paths in the woods in a normal way and then hit my head? So my brain sort of pieced things back together wrong? Hence him being a real, flesh-and-blood man, but also why I imagined we'd hooked up. We were just going to forget all about the whole wolf thing. Since, you know, that was insane.

"Your property?" he asked, brows drawing together. "I was under the impression that this land belonged to Greta Wilson."

"It did. Until she passed. And then it was given to me."

"Her granddaughter," he concluded.

"Yes. Maribelle. Mari," I said out of habit. My friends back home teased me about my full name, and always called me Mari instead. I actually liked my full name, but had accepted long ago that no one was going to use it. "Did you know my grandmother?" I asked, suddenly aching for some connection to her that didn't involve letters sent back and forth.

I'd been a shitty granddaughter for a long time. I mean, I always wrote. At least once a month, extra around the holidays or big life events. But I hadn't seen her face-to-face in years.

I would give just about anything to feel her hand—strong, thin, long-boned, knuckles a little knobby—grabbing my shoulder. That was as close as she got to a hug. But it always had the same effect to me, a child starved for adult attention and comfort.

As it turned out, I was now an *adult* starved for attention and comfort. I couldn't remember the last time someone gave my shoulder a squeeze, let alone hugged me.

Just the thought made annoying, unwanted tears sting at my eyes before I blinked them away as embarrassment flooded my system, hoping this hot Way guy didn't notice them.

He probably already thought I was insane since I clearly didn't remember meeting him. I didn't need to have a breakdown in front of him too.

"By reputation mostly," he admitted, giving me a bit of a smile that I felt myself returning, because I knew what he meant.

My grandmother was somewhat a legend in this little mountain town. She was the local recluse with a sharp wit and a filter-less mouth.

She didn't go into town often, so when she did, she packed her ancient pick-up truck to the gills with the essentials that she needed. Sugar. Coffee. Mason jar lids. And some hard candies, which had always been her one true vice. The house was full of jars of them. I hadn't been able to throw any of them away, just dusted them off and left them like decorations, like little tributes to her memory.

"She didn't exactly have a lot of friends," I admitted.

"No, she did not," Way agreed, and there was something in his voice, something almost, I don't know, dark. But it was gone before he spoke again, making me wonder if I'd been imagining it. "Are you here just to clean out, or…"

"Or," I admitted, not knowing why the hell I did so.

He was a random stranger.

In the woods.

At night.

Close to the cabin.

Like a creep.

He could be a rapist or something.

"Just me and my boyfriend," I lied. "He just retired from the NFL. We decided we wanted to come here for a bit of the mountain life before we decide what is next for us."

I am, in case this is not abundantly clear, an absolutely atrocious liar.

I mean… the NFL?

I could have said he was a construction worker or logger or something that required a lot of strength.

But nope.

I went with the least plausible option.

"The NFL, huh?" he asked.

"Yep." I mean, what choice did I have but to double-down at this point?

"What position?" he asked.

See, now, this is where lying about something you knew absolutely nothing about kind of worked against you.

"Oh, ah, he was, you know," I said, waving a hand out in front of me.

"A lineman?" Way supplied, looking thoroughly amused.

"Yes. That's it. Sorry. I think I must have hit my head really hard last night. I'm having… issues," I said, reaching up to touch the back of my head.

"Are you hurt?" he asked, his whole body tensing. "Do you need a doctor?" he added as he closed the space between us, one of his arms raising and going behind my head, landing on the crown.

And I swear a goddamn electrical current coursed through me. Not like static shock, either. Something stronger. Something that seemed to jolt through my entire system, making me suddenly hyperaware of his nearness, of his scent, of the heat emanating from his body.

Were people supposed to be that warm?

My arm felt suddenly full of lead, making it fall numbly by my side, leaving his hand pressing against my head instead, his big fingers surprisingly gentle as they probed my skin.

"Does this hurt?" he asked, gaze slipping to mine.

"I, ah…" Nope. In fact, it felt really, really freaking good to be touched. Even in such a chaste way. But I couldn't exactly tell him that, could I? What with my make-believe NFL boyfriend and all. "It's a little tender," I admitted.

"Have you been queasy? Lightheaded? Confused?"

"No. No. And… I guess. I'm having issues remembering last night correctly," I admitted. "Like, I feel like we met somehow. But then I think my brain sort of came up with a strange scenario on its own."

"Really?" he asked, brow quirking up. "What kind of scenario?" he asked.

I felt the heat spreading across my cheeks, and I didn't doubt that a blush was staining my cheeks.

"One where you were a wolf," I admitted. "And then you attacked me."

"Attacked you?" he asked, stiffening, seeming, I don't know, offended? Worried? Something like that.

"You like lunged at me and took me down. And then… you turned into a man again."

"What happened after I turned into a man again?" he asked, and I was suddenly aware that his hand had stopped probing, and his fingers were instead starting to gently massage my scalp.

I damn near melted.

Other girls could have the foot and back rubs. Those had never been my jam. But scalp rubs? I could damn near purr with pleasure right then and there.

Desire—pure, undiluted—pooled in my core, making me feel too sensitive to his touch, too aware of his closeness, the potential of his body and mine.

"I, ah, that's fuzzy," I lied as I tried not to whimper at the sensation as his fingers kept giving me exactly what I liked.

"Fuzzy," he repeated as his other hand raised, and both hands started to massage my scalp. "That's… unfortunate," he told me as his fingers pressed in just a little bit more, making my body sway into him, my chin falling down to give him more access. That he didn't need since he was so much taller than I was.

"Maribelle?" his voice purred, and I was so close that I felt the sound vibrate through his chest.

"Mmm?" I answered back, suddenly becoming aware that I felt the sounds he was making because my forehead was pressed to his chest.

Somehow, without being fully aware of it, I'd closed my eyes and leaned into him and almost drifted off to sleep.

"I don't think you have a serious head injury," he said.

And, suddenly, I managed to fully snap out of it.

If I thought I'd been blushing before, it was ten times worse right then as I yanked away from him, moving out of his arm's length because I almost felt, I don't know, entranced by the stranger.

Why else would I have let him rub my head?

"I, ah, I'm actually, you know, not so sure," I said, backing up more. "I'm going to go home now."

"To your lineman boyfriend?"

"What? Oh, yes. Yes, to my lineman boyfriend. He, ah, he must be wondering where I am," I babbled backing up more, then turning fully.

"Nice seeing you again, Maribelle," he called. And I went ahead and pretended that I didn't feel a little internal shiver at the way he said my name.

Instead, I just raised a hand in a half-hearted wave, and damn near ran back to the house, making sure I locked all the doors and windows before sitting down on the bed.

Even with some distance from him, that strange tug seemed to pull at me, and all my mind could think of was the way his hands had weaved magic, how he'd made me somehow made me feel completely safe and comforted by a complete stranger.

Not only that, but, well, he'd turned me on entirely. With such chaste, gentle contact.

Even the brush of my barely-there nightgown over my heated skin was enough to make a pained whimper escape me.

There was no way I was going to get any sort of rest with the unmet desire blazing through my system.

On a sigh, I rested back against the pillows on the bed, letting my hand drift up under my skirt, then moving between my thighs, finding myself already wet and needy.

Closing my eyes, I drifted back to the woods, melding both the fantasy and the reality together.

His hands in my hair, then his body over mine, and, finally, his face between my thighs.

That was how I knew it was pure fantasy.

What man had a willing woman and didn't slip inside her, didn't find his own release when she was more than happy to have him?

I let those thoughts slip away though, getting lost in the fantasies, in the ways my body was driving upward.

As I got higher and higher, I felt that strange tug, the same as before, but stronger. Almost, I don't know, closer.

But that was crazy.

Somehow, though, it made the sensations feel more acute until I was reaching that apex, then crashing down from the cliff.

I cried out at the intensity of the orgasm as it crashed and crashed through me in a seemingly never-ending wave, leaving me weak and exhausted afterward.

You'd think, after a rest like that, that I would sleep peacefully.

But I tossed and turned, waking up with fevered dreams full of howling wolves and soft fur and piercing brown eyes with flecks of yellow.

I woke up tired and frazzled, going around my morning tasks with a distracted mind and weirdly heated body, even with the cool autumn chill coming through the windows.

Frustrated, feeling like I was getting a bit of cabin fever, I moved out onto the front deck.

That was where I saw something that I was reasonably sure hadn't been there before.

Something sitting on the ledge of the bedroom window.

Curious, I made my way in that direction, finding some sort of rough gemstone sitting there. It was white but had some sort of iridescence when it caught the light.

I knew it.

A moonstone.

But where had it come from?

4

Waylon

Moonstone was naturally occurring in parts of Virginia.

There were flashier crystals around. The bright purple amethyst. The striking blue-green amanzonite. Hell, you could even find some garnet and topaz if you looked hard enough.

But there had always been something about moonstone for me. There was something poetic about it with our pack, with our connection to the moon.

I always had a piece or two in my pocket since I spent some of my free time digging for different gemstones. What can I say, when you spent almost all of your time in nature, you find new hobbies to keep you busy.

I hadn't meant to be creepy.

I'd just wanted to make sure she got home safely at first. And then I told myself that I just want to check to make sure that she wasn't crying again.

It couldn't be easy. Living all alone. I'd grown up with the pack. I'd never really known much solitude except when I was out in the woods.

People—and animals—were very rarely meant to live alone. It was unnatural. Community was important not only to survival, but morale.

Maribelle's breakdown on the porch was proof of that.

I just wanted to make sure she was okay. It wasn't really even much of a choice. The urge was somewhere deep inside, somewhere primal, somewhere decidedly wolf in nature.

I hadn't expected to look in and find her on the bed with her hand between her thighs, her back arching off the mattress, her breasts rising and falling with her labored breathing and her soft whimpers that grew to loud moans.

I couldn't seem to look away, to force myself to give her the privacy she had a right to.

Hell, I couldn't even stop my own fucking hand from slipping into my pants and grabbing my cock, from bringing myself to a leg-weakening orgasms just as she found her own.

I was left with my face pressed to the wood of the cabin, trying to catch my breath afterward.

Inside, Maribelle seemed equally afflicted.

Eventually, I pulled out the moonstone, leaving it there as a little keepsake, as proof that I'd been there, as a present for her to have, to keep with her.

Since I couldn't be.

At least not yet.

My plan was to weasel my way in, to start finding ways to be near her, to get to know her, to feel her out and see if she was like her grandmother, or if she was someone I could truly trust.

My pack was probably going to have questions. Which was why I was concocting a lie as I made my way through the woods and back to our campsite.

"What kind of retreat?" Garrick asked.

He was closest in age to me, with a little bit of silver streaking its way into his medium-brown hair. He had some crinkles next to his green eyes. I had ones just like it.

The old guys, that was what we were.

The bad example.

The cautionary tale.

About not finding your True Mate. About not securing a future for us, for our bloodlines, for our pack.

"It's just a wellness retreat, of sorts. I've been feeling pretty distracted, lost in my head lately. I think I just need a week alone in nature to get grounded."

"It can get loud here," Garrick agreed, looking around at the other guys milling around. "I'll miss you, brother," he said. "But I understand. Make sure you bring extra of everything."

With that, I did.

I packed a tent full of the essentials—clothes, cooking supplies, personal hygiene, some blankets—and then I made my way into the woods, heading back toward the cabin, but setting up deep and high enough that she would not see me, but I could see her cabin, keep an eye on her.

And, slowly but surely, become a part of her world, someone she could trust, someone to open up to.

Then I could get to know her.

I could see if my future was her.

I had to admit as I set up camp, that I wanted it to be.

Not just because I was desperate to fine my True Mate or because I wanted my own children. Though both those things were true.

But I was also just intrigued by her. By her beauty. By her decision to move out into the woods.

I wanted to know why.

I wanted to know what her life was like before.

She seemed both familiar with the mountains and the woods, and also out of her depths with them.

Getting lost alone in the woods at night was not great. Sure, predators were few and far between in the area because our pack kept them away, but she didn't know that.

My mind was on those things the following morning as I watched a pathetic puff of smoke start out of the chimney then die out. Not a couple minutes later, the door opened, and there was Maribelle dressed in a baggy sweater with a scarf wrapped around her head, walking over to the side of the house where a firewood storage box was located.

She lifted up the tarp, and must have found it empty, because her shoulders sagged.

It wasn't that cool yet, but living using fireplaces instead of forced hot air probably took a bit of getting used to. There were just nooks and crannies in a home where the heat simply didn't get to. Sometimes the chill could creep in between the fabrics of your clothes, leaving you chilled.

Taking a deep breath, Maribelle looked over at the pile of logs that her grandmother must have managed to procure or fell herself before she passed.

She could have gone back in the cabin. Put on another layer or two. Made a cup of tea to warm up from the inside.

Those would be things that a woman who wasn't planning on staying would do.

But she didn't do those things.

She went in search of the ax and then made her way over to the wood, piling a smaller piece on the chopping block, taking a couple of practice swings, then chopping.

I mean… she missed completely.

But that wasn't exactly the point.

She tried.

It counted for something.

That was the kind of partner you wanted. One who was willing to work, willing to try.

Going back into my tent, I grabbed the little welcome basket I'd put together before leaving the camp, and made my way toward the path, so she would see me coming, so it didn't look like I was being a creep again.

She was valiantly chipping off little pieces of the log with another swing when she saw me coming.

I swear I could feel the relief as it washed over her.

"Hey," she called as I got closer.

"Hey, neighbor," I said. "If my mother was still around, she'd tan my hide if she knew I greeted the new neighbor and didn't bring them a welcome basket," I told her, waving the pack with snacks and a bottle of wine at her. "You need some help with that?" he asked, trying to keep from smirking as I saw that she'd somehow managed to wedge the ax into the chopping block instead of the log.

"Don't laugh," she demanded, even though she was letting out a small chuckle at her own expense. "I am city folk," she said, taking the basket from me. "The closest thing to manual labor I needed to do in the city was raising my arm to hail a cab."

"How about I cut a couple logs up for you?" I asked, but it was more of a demand, because I was already reaching for the handle of the ax.

"If you insist," he said, glad to step away.

"Where's that no-good boyfriend of yours?" I asked as I swung the ax down and split the log, noticing the way her pretty lips fell open, not used to seeing men do manly shit.

"I, ah, I have to confess to something…" she said, eyeing me.

"That you made up the lineman boyfriend lie because you were worried I was a creep?" I asked, shooting her a devilish little smile.

To that, an all-too-appealing blush crept across her cheeks and nose.

"I'm a terrible liar," she admitted, shaking her head.

"Baby, that's not a bad trait to have," I said, shrugging it off, pretending I didn't sense the way desire pinged through her body at the pet name.

Pet names and scalp massages. That was what this woman liked best so far.

"I guess. I mean, I once tried to get out of going to a work event by saying I'd broken my ankle. I, um, had to put a fake cast on for weeks after," she admitted. "I was never so glad to go remote."

"Remote," I repeated. "Sounds like a synonym for lonely."

Her brows lifted at that. "Ah, yeah, I guess. It's hard to believe that in a city of like eight million people that you can feel alone, but yeah."

"Way I see it, it's probably worse."

"What do you mean?" she asked as I propped up another piece of wood.

"If you're going through some shit and need someone, passing by hundreds or thousands of people each day who don't care that you exist, that shit can make someone feel really invisible and insignificant."

"That's... that is exactly it," she said, nodding.

"Hey, Maribelle?" I called as I grabbed another log.

"Yeah?"

"You're not insignificant."

It was a nothing thing to say. But it was something she clearly needed to hear. Because tears flooded her eyes for a second before she rapidly blinked them away. But not before one managed to slip out.

Feeling it, she reached out, pretending to scratch her face to disguise the fact that she was wiping it away.

"I have to admit that I feel pretty insignificant that I can't even keep myself warm," she said, waving at my small stack of wood I'd already split.

"Hey, this shit? This is nothing. Just takes some practice and determination. You'll get there. In the meantime, I don't mind."

"I can't just ask you to come here every couple days and split wood for me."

"Why not?" I asked, shrugging.

"Why not? Because, ah, that's a big inconvenience."

"It's not."

"You have a life."

"This only takes a short hour out of it," I shot back.

"I should be able to take care of myself," she said, crossing her arms over her chest, a defensive gesture.

"Who made you believe that?" I asked, softening my voice. "There's nothing wrong with leaning on someone else's strengths so you have the time and freedom to lean into your own."

I could have sworn she mumbled *What strengths* under her breath, but she clearly didn't want me to hear that.

"So is this your first time in the area?" I asked, wanting to lighten the mood.

"No. I mean, it's the first time in a long time. But I used to spend every summer here when I was a young girl."

"Really?"

"Yeah. My parents, well, is there a nice way to say they probably shouldn't have had children? They didn't want to have to deal with me full-time when school was out, so they shipped me down here to my grandmother. Which was for the best. I have some of my fondest memories here. But then…"

"You became a punk-ass teenager who thought you were too cool for summers with your gran?" I asked, getting another little laugh out of her.

"Something like that, yeah. I really regret that now. And that I didn't visit when I could have as an adult. We kept in touch, but she wouldn't be caught dead in the city, and I always thought it would be too much of a hassle or a bore to be out here. Do you know there is, like, no cell reception? And forget about wifi."

"Yeah, folks 'round here tend to spend more time outdoors or with friends and family. We kinda like it that way."

"That's why I'm here. Well, partly. To, you know, see if I like it that way."

"What's the other part of why you're here then?"

"Well, it ties into the first part. If I decide the whole gardening and living off the land thing isn't for me, at least it gives me some time away from the craziness of the city to figure out what I do want the future to hold."

"So you quit your old job?"

"For the time being, I'm on leave. I can work remote from here if I can find a way to get the wifi to work."

"You can stay here then?" I asked, praying the hope wasn't too clear in my voice. "If you decide you like gardening and shit," I clarified.

"Yeah. I mean, I'm sure my company will want me in for a meeting on occasion, but it isn't that far that I can't do that once or twice a year if I have to. But I don't think I want to do that forever. It's a big part of the reason I felt like I needed to come here. And why I put on fifty pounds," she grumbled, mostly to herself. "All the misery weight."

"Well, maybe you can find some joy here and keep those pounds on as happy weight," I suggested, letting my gaze roam over her for just long enough that it was clear I liked what I was seeing, without it being creepy as fuck.

"I thought the whole point of living off the land was to be lean and muscly."

"Sometimes curves are superior to hard lines," I said, grabbing another log.

"God, you can stop that. You've done like half of that pile already," she said.

"In the absence of more fun ways, we gotta keep you warm, don't we?" I asked, watching as her eyelids went a little heavy at the insinuation.

"How cold does it get here in the winter anyway?" she asked.

"Can be in the mid to high thirties. Especially up this way."

"I'm going to need a lot more wood," she grumbled, looking at her empty storage.

"Your gran died in the spring, right?" I asked.

"Yeah."

"It's why it's so empty. She would have spent the whole summer stocking up."

"I could get a delivery of wood," Meribelle said.

"You could," I agreed. "But I'd be happy to show you the ropes so you can get your own. There's no shortage of trees around here. And you still have some time. If you end up not liking it, I can put you in touch with a crew who does wood."

She didn't have to know that it was a speciality of my pack.

What can I say? We liked the outdoors. And we were happiest when we worked jobs that kept us in it.

"What?" I asked, catching her staring at me.

"You know I lived in my apartment for three years in the city. I never even had a conversation with my neighbors. Well, one of the neighbors dogs. He and I were good friends in the hallway and elevator. But not the actual people."

"That's sad, babe."

"I'm starting to see that. Okay. Really, that's enough for one day. You've been so helpful. Can I, ah, make you a cup of coffee?"

To get in her cabin with her?

Abso-fucking-lutely.

"Sounds good," I said. "Run ahead. I'll bring some of this in."

The cabin itself was a small area, likely built that way because it was easier to keep it warm in the winters with just the central fireplace. There was a kitchen to the side wall and then the common area that was cluttered with overflowing bookshelves, couches, and remnants of what looked like knitting and quilting projects.

There was an open door to the bedroom with its queen-sized bed with an antique bronze frame and layers and layers of brightly-colored quilts.

That was, if I recalled correctly, how her grandmother had made her income. Selling quilts in town. Everyone was always looking for a custom baby blanket or a wedding gift or just to have something pretty and fancy on their own beds.

"Aren't they gorgeous?" Maribelle asked, noticing me looking at them. "My grandmother had such a gift with them. I was learning when I was a girl. I actually made that one she hung on the wall," she said, waving over toward the space between the bedroom and bathroom where a bright pink and yellow doll-sized blanket was displayed like a prize possession.

"I want to learn again. I forgot how to use the machine, but I found the book and I'm working on it. Maybe I can make you a big blanket one day to thank you for being such a good neighbor."

"I'd fucking love that," I told her, watching as she went a little pink again.

This woman had clearly been starved for attention and affection and just common courtesy for far too fucking long.

I planned to change that.

"What are your favorite colors?" she asked as she grabbed two mugs from the cupboard.

"Green is my favorite. Go with your gut for the other colors," I said.

"How do you take it?" she asked, holding up cream and sugar.

"Yes cream. No sugar."

"Don't judge me for taking your portion of sugar then," she said, making up the cups, then holding mine out to me.

Did I go ahead and make sure that my fingers brushed hers as I took it? Damn right I did.

And that sizzle at the contact was only reinforcing what I already knew down to my core.

It was her.

She was the one.

I just had no idea if she was going to feel the same for me.

5

Maribelle

I could get used to having Way around.

Ever since the day with the woods, when I'd woken up from a nap that I was worried was speaking of a upcoming depression spell, to a frigid home.

I mean, yes, admittedly, I always ran a little cold. My hands and feet were icicles no matter how hot the external temperature. I spent much of the summer bundled up in oversized hoodies and thick socks, no matter how warm I kept my apartment.

When I'd finally figured out the fireplace, and found no wood to fuel it with, I'd felt a surge of helplessness that made me want to throw up my hands and say "screw it" and head back to the city. Where I never had to do any sort of labor to make my heat or air work.

But that was the whole point of coming to the cabin, wasn't it? To force myself to live a different way, to help change my perspective, to shake things up.

I couldn't run away at the first sign of struggle.

Admittedly, though, I damn near did when I couldn't even split a log properly, a task my eighty-something-year-old grandmother had been doing for herself.

Then there he was.

With a welcome basket full of wine and treats. And an offering to help.

I almost cried.

Like… I actually did. A tear or two before I pulled myself together.

I'd never truly understood the appeal of a sort of traditional "alpha" type of man.

I liked men who were forward-thinking and in touch with their feelings. In other words… guys who weren't misogynists. I'd never met a self-proclaimed "alpha man" who didn't think that women were just holes to be stuffed and hands to make them dinner.

Then again, I guess Way had never called himself that. He just exuded it.

In a classic sort of way.

The way that said he was happy to do the manual labor, to help women, maybe even protect them if they needed that.

We'd had a nice hour or so chat over coffee, talking about my life in the city, the fact that he'd never really been far from this area of Virginia, about his favorite outdoor pastimes, and my love of books.

Then he'd said his goodbyes, and I stood there watching him from the window as he disappeared into the woods.

I'd never felt such a strong sense of loss as I watched him go.

And I convinced myself for the rest of that day that it was just because I was so alone. Which was completely absurd. Because while, yes, people were all around in the city, I was every bit as alone there as I was in this cabin.

I woke up the next morning to the rhythmic sound of wood chopping, and got up to look out my window to find him there at the side of the house with a pile of logs there that hadn't been there the day before.

Had he… cut down trees for me? Then dragged them to the cabin and started chopping them?

Oh, did I mention he had his shirt off?

No, not just like… open.

Nope.

The green flannel was bunched up and sitting next to the pile of chopped wood.

And, ah, yeah, somehow he was exactly how my fantasies had painted him without his shirt on.

Again, those weird concussion dreams flashed across my vision, and I knew exactly what that skin felt like, pulled taut over firm muscles.

As if sensing me, he straightened, his head turning over in my direction, giving me a soft smile.

Feeling caught, I jerked away from the window and made my way into the kitchen, putting on a pot of coffee to bring him out as a thank you, then slipping on shoes and one of my grandmother's warm shawls to partially cover my thin nightgown that was definitely more pretty than practical.

I was going to go ahead and not analyze why I was suddenly wearing pretty nightgowns to bed when my usual nighttime attire was sweatpants and oversized tees or sweatshirts.

As soon as I made my way around the corner of the house, Way was swinging the ax down into a big log.

My mouth went dry.

And other parts of me, well, *dry* was not the problem.

Almost as if he sensed my thoughts, his body stiffened and he turned to look at me.

Was that heat in his eyes?

The way my body warmed said it was.

"Hey," I said, feeling dumb, like I should have come up with something to say while I waited for the coffee to drip.

"I didn't mean to wake you," he said, tone soft as I held out his mug to him.

"How long have you been here?" I asked, looking at his progress.

"Couple hours," he told me, shrugging it off.

"It's barely eight," I said, shaking my head.

"I get up early. There's a cold snap coming. I wanted to make sure you have enough wood to keep you warm," he told me, and I swear his gaze dipped down to my chest where my nipples were pebbled up hard against the thin material.

"That is really sweet," I said. Because it was. Because I couldn't say what I was really thinking.

Which was something about riding him until we both came hard.

"Just being a halfway decent guy, baby," he said, shaking his head.

"Do you know how many men I've had not hold a door for me?" I asked. "Trust me, this is more than halfway decent."

"They may have been males, but those were not men," Way said, looking disgusted on my behalf. "How was your night?" he asked as he drained his too-hot coffee, putting the mug down on the wood pile.

"It was good. The fire really helped."

"You're cold," he said as the wind kicked up, making a shiver course through me.

Then this man grabbed his discarded flannel and brought it over to me.

"Here," he said, pulling it behind my back, settling it on my shoulders, but holding the material by the sides, his warm fingertips touching my frigid skin above the deep square-neck of my nightgown. The touch and his nearness made an entirely different kind of shiver move through me. "There are other ways to warm up," he said, voice lower, deeper.

"Really?" I asked, looking up at him, my chest getting tight, my thighs clenching together to try to ease the ache there.

With a small yank of the material, he forced my whole front to his whole front.

"Oh," I said, the sound part surprise and part disappointment. There was no denying I thought he meant something else entirely. "You're so hot," I said, then felt my cheeks heat at the way that could be taken. "Warm. You're so warm." Though, yeah, he was undoubtedly hot as well.

One of his hands rose, grabbing the back of my neck, applying pressure until my head rested against his chest, where I took a deep breath of his unique scent. Something woodsy and masculine.

It was practically narcotic.

I felt oddly drunk off of just the scent of him.

"Better?" he asked, his chest vibrating into mine, making my breasts feel heavy, desperate for touch.

"Mmhm," I said, not caring how that sounded.

I didn't seem entirely capable of rational thought right then.

I felt completely and thoroughly… consumed by him.

I mean, closeness with a guy you were attracted to was always kind of intense.

But nothing in my life had ever felt quite like this.

It was overwhelming.

I felt like I might cry if he didn't touch me.

As if sensing that thought, his other hand lifted, anchoring around my back, holding me tightly against him as the other hand shifted up, and his fingers started to gently massage my scalp.

I didn't purr.

But the sound that came out of me then, well, it was, you know, purr-like.

And that sound made a delicious little growling sound move through Way's chest, vibrating into mine.

Suddenly, his fingers turned, grabbing a handful of my hair, and gently yanking me back by it until I had no choice but to angle my head up to look at him.

His dark eyes searched my face for a moment.

He must have found what he was looking for then, because his lips crashed down on mine.

Hard.

Hungry.

Bruising.

And I just… melted into him.

I became suddenly aware of every inch of my body somehow at the same time. The crush of my breasts to his chest. His strong fingers holding my head. The arm crushing across my back. The throbbing ache between my thighs.

All of it, though, seemed oddly eclipsed by something else, something that grew from somewhere buried deep, some sort of overwhelming feeling of rightness, of oneness.

I didn't even have a name for it, had never experienced anything even close to it in the past.

All I knew was there was something comforting about it, so despite not even having a clue what it was, I leaned into it, into him.

I melted in his arms, feeling him wrap me up tighter as he kissed me like it was a promise of forever, like it followed a vow at an altar and rings exchanged.

My arms went up, wrapping around his neck, his skin warm under my fingers despite the chill around us.

Even when his hands slipped downward, gathering up my skirt and exposing my ass, I didn't feel anything but the brush of his heated skin, but the pang of desire as his hands sank into my ass, using it to pin me against his hips where his cock was hard and straining for me already.

Everything just felt very… familiar. And because of that familiarity, comfortable.

Suddenly, Way's hands were sinking in hard to my ass, dragging me up and off my feet by it until I wrapped my legs around his waist, holding on for dear life as he started to move.

I'd never been carried by a man.

But Way had lifted me up like it was nothing.

I never expected just how hot it was to have a man that strong, but there was no denying it was just amplifying the need already consuming me.

The next thing I knew, my ass was dropping down on the top of the porch railing that I didn't exactly have a lot of faith in.

Way seemed oblivious to this, though, as he yanked away from me to drop down onto his knees, slipping up under my skirt, and teasing his lips up my thigh.

Again… familiar.

The way he kissed, the scrape of his stubble.

So very much like that fantasy that had been playing around in my head.

But then his face was between my thighs, tracing up my cleft, and toying with my clit, and all those pesky, rational thoughts? Yeah, they flew right out of my head. And good riddance. Who needed them, when you had a gorgeous man licking and sucking and teasing you with his tongue and lips and the barest scrape of his teeth?

Not me.

I got enveloped in the sensations as he teased over me, driving me up, as he slipped two fingers into my waiting heat, as he stroked with perfect rhythm, then turned and started to glide against my top wall as his tongue moved a little faster on my clit.

"Not yet," he hissed, mouth ripping from me as I let out a pained moan. "I need you to come around my cock," he told me.

And never, absolutely never before, did I want to feel a man inside me as much as I wanted to feel him.

His hands sank into my hips as he got to his feet, pulling me off the shaky railing, then turning me so my back met his chest.

I wasn't even fully aware of telling my hands to hike up my skirt, to offer a silent invitation, but that was exactly what I did.

Way's hands went around me, though, finding a little more patience, just enough to pull down the neckline of my bodice and expose my breasts to the chilly air.

His hands covered them immediately, squeezing the swells, then rolling my nipples between his thumbs and forefingers until I was writhing, until I was grinding back against his straining cock.

"I need to be inside you," he growled in my ear, his voice deliciously deep. It made a shiver course through my core.

"Yes. Please," I whimpered, pressing my thighs together to ease the ache there.

On a vibrating rumble, he reached behind me, freeing himself.

I felt him tease against my cleft, rubbing at my wetness, then pressing against me.

His one arm went around my chest, anchoring me to his body as he surged inside me.

A deep moan escaped me as he filled me completely, perfectly, entirely.

"Mine," he growled in my ear, his voice rough.

Mine?

That was… that was definitely what he said.

And that was what the dream version of him had said as well.

How could he have possibly known that?

Before I could even let those thoughts take root, though, he was moving inside of me.

Slowly at first, letting me adjust, then harder, faster. His hips and cock and the hand that went between my thighs were all demanding, insisting, I give them what they were seeking.

I don't think I'd ever been driven up quite so quickly before.

It felt like just a few short moments before I was pressed to that edge, was teetering there, about to fall over, to crash down.

"Come for me. Squeeze my cock," he growled in my ear as he kept thrusting, kept teasing my clit. "Make me yours," I could have sworn he added, his voice barely more than a whisper.

But something inside of me responded.

And then I was falling and the waves of pleasure were washing over me again and again, until I felt like I couldn't catch my breath, until my legs didn't seem capable of holding me up anymore.

"*Mine*," Way hissed as he slammed deep, coming at the tail-end of my orgasm.

I couldn't say how long we stayed exactly that way, his arms holding me up since my body refused to cooperate, trying to catch out breaths, trying to come to terms with what had happened.

And what had happened was… I'd let him inside of me… without even seeing if he had protection on.

Oh, God.

I mean, I was on hormones so that I didn't end up pregnant, but that wasn't exactly the only thing you had to worry about.

"Baby," Way's voice called, soft, sweet, his lips brushing my ear as he spoke. "Don't regret me," he added, making my heart squeeze in my chest.

"I don't," I assured him, because I was sure it wasn't even possible to regret the feelings we'd just shared, the bliss he'd just given me.

"No?" he asked.

"No," I told him as I felt him reach for my chin, turning it just enough so his lips could brush mine.

"Good," he told me between soft kisses. "I couldn't live with that," he added.

That seemed… dramatic.

And yet something inside of me responded. My belly fluttered. My heart squeezed.

Like it was somehow, I don't know, right.

Which was what I'd felt in the woods when…

Mine.

"What's wrong?" Way asked as I suddenly yanked away from him.

I tucked my breasts away before turning to face him, finding that he'd tucked himself away as well.

I knew what he saw reflected in my eyes.

Accusation.

"You lied to me," I hissed, raking a hand through my hair.

"Maribelle…"

"I didn't just… I didn't just run into you. You… we… you did things," I said, voice choked.

I saw the truth on his face even before he opened his mouth to confirm it.

"Yes."

"You let me think I had, like, brain damage, that I'd imagined it all. Why would you do that? Who does that!"

I yanked my arm away when he tried to reach out to me, some base, primal part of me knowing that if he touched me, I would lose all rational thought again.

"Let me explain," he implored.

"You know what? No. No, I don't think so. Go," I demanded, waving out toward the yard. "Leave," I said, trying to put more emphasis into the words.

He tried to take another step toward me, and I must have flinched, because I watched him shrink into himself in response, then turn and do as I demanded.

I swear, as insane as this sounded, each step he took away from me was like a stabbing sensation to the gut.

Not trusting myself not to run to him, to ease the ache, I forced myself inside the cabin, closing, then locking the door.

It wasn't until I got to the bathroom that I realized tears had filled my eyes and started to spill down my cheeks.

"Stupid. So stupid," I hissed to my reflection as I wiped the tears away, not entirely understanding their presence.

I mean, yeah, I'd been starting to really like Way. But so what? I'd liked plenty of guys who turned out to be douchebags in the past.

This felt different, though.

It felt like someone had sliced a part of me out.

It made no sense.

I barely knew the guy.

I mean, I didn't know him at all if he'd been lying to me pretty much since we'd met.

It was stupid to be so upset.

I was just… overly lonely. Isolated. Unsure of my future.

And he'd been nice to me.

I was needy enough that I didn't seem to require anything other than that.

"Pathetic," I told my reflection before I turned, stripped out of my nightgown, and climbed in the tub, letting the frigid water wash over me as punishment while I scrubbed mercilessly at my skin.

Like I could wash away the feel of him.

It was unsuccessful.

And, somehow, the time only seemed to amplify the sadness and strange feeling of incompleteness that had been there since he'd walked away.

I tried to get some things done inside the house, to distract myself, to think of literally anything else.

Unsuccessful, I climbed into bed, pulled the cover over my head, and slept.

I thought I was dreaming it again at first.

Until I was startled fully awake.

And I knew it wasn't a dream.

It was reality.

And it was eerily close.

A lone wolf's howl.

I leaped out of bed, rushing toward the window, and looking out into the yard.

Then there it was.

Just like the one from my dream.

Standing a few feet off from the front porch, his big head tossed back, his mouth forming a little *O* as he bellowed.

My hand rose to the glass, settling it there as if I could touch its fur, could feel it sifting through my fingers.

A strange fantasy, to be sure.

As if sensing my presence, he stopped suddenly, and his yellowish eyes pinned me in my place.

Some strange part of me wanted to rush out, wanted to reach out and touch him.

But seeing as he was a, you know, freaking *wolf*—and a massive one at that—I went ahead and backed away from the window.

I stayed close enough, though, to watch him.

And what did he do?

He paced.

Right in front of the front porch.

Over and over and over, his gaze slipping from watching the darkness, to glancing back at me.

What did I do?

I watched him.

All night long.

Until the moon was finally starting to go down, and the sun was stretching its fingers across the sky.

Only then did he look back at me, walk up onto the porch, lean down almost as if he was dropping something, then looked at me, and ran off.

I watched him as he went, his massive body practically flying into the woods with his long strides.

Then I went ahead and waited an extra couple of minutes to make sure he wasn't still hanging around and cracked open the front door to see why he'd been on the porch.

And there it was.

Another of those milky, slightly iridescent crystals. Like the one I'd found on my window ledge.

A wolf had… brought me a present?

I was no wildlife expert, but that seemed, abnormal, right?

What was perhaps even more abnormal, though, was that I took the rock to bed with me to take a nap, sleeping away the day, just so I could get up and see if my wolf came back the next night.

Or the fact that my heart seemed to swell in my chest when I saw him come walking out of the woods to pace my porch yet again.

What the hell was going on?

6

Waylon

I anticipated the pain.

From all the stories that were passed down to us through the generations, we all knew that the pain of a rejected mate was something intense, something you never wanted to experience.

I hadn't expected for it to feel like a thousand daggers stabbing me all over my body with each step I took away from that house, away from her.

All because I'd fucking lied to her, been secretive with her.

But what was I supposed to tell her? That I'd been in my most primal form when I'd first sensed her? That I'd lost control of the beast within me and damn near assaulted her in the woods?

Then left her there.

Unsure.

Alone.

How was that any better than letting her believe she'd hit her head and imagined it all?

I'd wanted a fresh start, to build a relationship with her, to find some trust. Then I planned to explain it all.

I was always going to tell her the full story.

When the time felt right.

I thought I'd get the chance to get there.

What a huge fucking mistake.

I barely made it to the woods before the Change took over me.

I dropped to my knees in the dirt and pine needles as the wolf tore his way out of me.

I flew through the woods, trying to outrun the pain, but it got worse and worse the further I went until I had no choice but to give in, to go back to the cabin.

I paced and howled and whined.

Then I felt her.

The urge to burst through the front door, to feel her again, was so strong I'd barely been able to hold myself off.

I'd never felt anything like the pain I felt even in my wolf form as I was only a few yards from her, knowing I would likely never get to have her again.

That fact didn't change the bond, it didn't shake the need to be near her, to protect her.

The way she watched me was the only thing giving me any hope.

For as long as I paced—all night—she was somewhere in the cabin watching me.

Finally, I felt the dawn coming, so I left her the stone, then made my way back to my camp, writhing in pain until sleep finally claimed me.

And so the cycle went for a few days.

My pacing.

Her watching.

Until, on the fourth day, the door slid open, and there she was.

The smell of her almost overpowered me.

The chorus of the animal inside of me chanted over and over *Mine mine mine mine mine.*

She said nothing, just watched me with guarded, but curious eyes as she took one step out, then another.

She left the door open behind her, giving herself an escape should she decide I was feral and ready to kill her.

Meanwhile every fiber of my being thrummed with the need to protect her. At all costs. At even the risk of my own life.

I'd happily lay down my very existence for her. I knew it down to my bones.

I kept my body completely still as she kept making careful progress across the front porch.

When she got down to the lowest step, I bowed my head at her, showing submission, reassuring her I meant no harm.

Her hand rose slowly, stretching outward, then touching me just behind my ear, her fingers stroking through my fur. Just a whisper at first, then sinking in and rubbing as she got more comfortable, as she became sure she was safe.

"You're beautiful," she murmured, her voice soft, full of admiration and awe. "What have you been doing here every night, huh? Doesn't some pretty wolf-lady miss you?" she asked.

I couldn't seem to stop the huff that escaped me at that.

Like there was anyone in the world but her. Like it was possible to ever look at another woman again.

"No ladies, huh? Well, that sucks, huh?" she asked as she carefully lowered herself down onto the step.

Following her lead, I sat, wanting to keep her comfortable.

"You're almost… tame," she said, reaching out with her other hand, both of them starting to stroke over my coat. "I don't understand why you're here. But I have to admit I'm kind of glad you are. I've been so alone," she added, feeling comfortable being vulnerable because she had no way of knowing I could understand.

Even if I couldn't, the misery was bouncing off of her. Any beast could feel it. Not just those of us who were only half-beast.

"It's hard to be alone, right?" she asked, leaning forward a bit, pressing her forehead to mine. "Thanks for being here," she whispered. "I've gotten kind of used to having you around. It sounds kind of crazy, but I feel like my heart would shatter in a thousand little pieces if you weren't around."

I didn't think about it.

I moved forward, waiting for her to take the hint and scoot back, then sprawling across her lap, warming her, comforting her, and being as close as we both needed.

She said nothing else for the rest of the night. Just stroked her hands over me.

And then I felt it.

The first rays of light.

"I know," she whispered, feeling me shift. "You have to go. Thanks for sitting with me, though. I feel better," she said, leaning down to press a kiss to my head, then getting to her feet, and watching me go.

As soon as it was safe to do so, I Changed back, watching her as she stood on the porch for a long moment, her beautiful eyes scanning the tree line before she moved inside to get some much-needed rest.

I sat with her again the next night, but this time, she'd invited me into the cabin, both of us warming by the fire as she stroked my fur and talked about her life in the city, and her concerns that maybe she wasn't cut out for life in the woods all alone.

"You are making it a lot better," she told me, patting my head like she was reassuring me. "But I am a little worried that you are acting more like a lapdog than a wild wolf. Like, should I be feeding you? Can you catch your own food? What do you even like to eat? Just raw meat, right? Gross. I mean, I'm not judging. I just couldn't do it.

"I should probably head into town soon and find a shrink, huh? This is probably not a normal, rational person's behavior."

But she just kept talking to me until the morning, when she led me toward the door, and said she would see me the next night.

Which was the plan.

Until I was roaming the woods, gathering some supplies for my camp, wasting time until I could go see her again.

And I heard a scream.

Her scream.

I never Changed so fast in my life.

I hadn't been watching the house, figuring she would be sleeping until late.

So I had no idea where she'd gone, what had befallen her.

So I had to get into my wolf form to be able to smell her, to track her, to make sure she was okay.

I sprinted through the woods, following her sweet scent as I got closer and closer.

I found her not far from her house wearing her crappy hiking boots and athleisure that hugged all her perfect curves, looking like she'd decided to get out in nature and take a walk, likely feeling cooped up for being in the house so much lately.

She'd been trying to scale a small rock formation, likely wanting to head up in the direction of the river that ran that way.

But her foot must have slipped, sending her falling back down, landing on the ground where I found her, clutching her leg with both her hands, her whole body rocking as she whimpered.

"Ow ow ow ow ow. Damnit. That's what I get for trying to get active. Now I'll die out here and get eaten by scavengers. Oh, ow," she cried as she tried to move the leg.

Moving forward, my paw hit a twig, making it crunch.

Maribelle's head snapped up, eyes huge, worried, before her face settled a bit.

"It's you," she said, exhaling hard before her voice hitched and a choked sob escaped her. "Listen, you have to stop being so loyal. I'm going to slip a leash on you and force you to live with me," she said, wiping her cheeks.

I couldn't help her in my wolf form.

And judging by the way she couldn't seem to move, let alone put any weight on her leg, she was not going to get back home on her own.

Maybe it was time.

And even if perhaps it wasn't the best time, there didn't seem to be any other option.

Taking a deep breath, waiting for her gaze to find me again, I let the Change take over me, going back to my human form right before her eyes.

There was a long pause as she stared at me.

"I might not be averse to that living situation," I told her.

"I knew it," she said, shaking her head. "I mean, I didn't know-it, know it. How could I? But I… you… it was the only time it didn't hurt," she said, eyes more vulnerable than I'd ever seen them.

"I know, baby. I've been feeling it too," I assured her, reaching out, placing a hand on top of hers, giving it a gentle squeeze.

"But… why?"

"Because we're mates," I told her.

"Mates?"

"Yeah, True Mates, to be exact."

"I don't understand," she admitted.

"Didn't you feel it? Almost from the very beginning? The rightness."

"I… sort of. I guess. I still don't understand. What are True Mates?"

"Something like soulmates. But even deeper than that."

"What is deeper than the soul?"

"The very fibers of your being. Didn't you feel it? Like we were tied together. Like everything was wrong when we weren't close."

"Y…yes. I mean, I thought I was going crazy. Or getting depressed. I mean, I was confessing all my darkest secrets to a wolf that I let into my house where he could have easily eaten me."

"The kind of eating I have in mind is a little different than the kind you mean," I told her, watching as that cute as fuck blush crept over her cheeks.

"So… you're a… ah… werewolf?"

"We tend to use the term shifter these days. Werewolves have weird ties to bullshit lies made up by movie and TV creators. But, yes. I have a wolf side."

"And when you're a wolf… do you, you know, think like a wolf?"

"Somewhat, yes. There's a more animalistic drive. But I am also me in there as well."

"What does it mean if I am your True Mate?"

"There's no if about it, baby. You are. I feel it in my bones, in my marrow. You're mine. But as for what happens, that's… up to you."

"Up to me how?"

"Well, you can accept me. And then there would be no more pain. Or you can reject me. You'll feel pain that will eventually dull. You'd go on to live a normal, human life."

"And you?"

"And I… would be driven mad by the pain. Until, eventually, I would probably let the wolf overtake me completely, so I no longer have to feel it."

"What? Are you serious? That can happen?"

"That has happened, yes," I told her, exhaling hard. "That is part of the reason I haven't been fully honest with you from the beginning. Because of history."

"What history?"

"The history between my pack… and your grandmother."

"My grandmother?" she hissed, back straightening. "What about my grandmother?"

"Many, many years ago, your grandmother was proven to be the True Mate of one of my pack. When she rejected him, he was driven insane from the pain. He became a wolf. Then eventually he jumped over a cliff to his death. He was our alpha, our leader," I added, knowing from my own father how deep that pain had cut the entire pack, how it had scattered us, leaving some to break off and form their own packs, becoming rivals to their once-brothers.

"Wait…no. No way. She never…"

"Baby, I wouldn't lie about this. It's true."

"Would she have known he was a were… shifter?"

"It was before my time. I'm not sure. Either way, she didn't want anything to do with him. And whether or not she understood what was happening, it had repercussions that still rock my pack to this day. So I was… hesitant."

"That I would be like her?" she asked, waiting for my nod. "Do you ever think that maybe… maybe he just wasn't a good man?" she asked.

"Maybe he wasn't kind and generous and sweet. Maybe he treated her poorly."

"We can't hurt you. It would hurt us too."

"But it was a different time. My grandmother… she was… difficult. She had a bad history with men and wanted nothing to do with one again. If your alpha was trying to make her settle down, I could have seen her pushing him further away. Not because she wanted to hurt him, but because she'd been so hurt in the past.

"But either way, it was kind of silly to assume that just because she rejected a mate, that I would as well. We're different people."

"Didn't know that about her," I said, shrugging. "I just wanted to make sure about you before I told you about everything."

"Then, of course, there's the fact that a sane person doesn't believe in were…shifters," she said, shooting me a smirk.

"There's that, yeah," I agreed.

"Do you guys always find your mate with, you know, humans?"

"For as far back as I can remember. Female wolves are so rare that I've never met one."

"So your whole pack is…"

"Men," I supplied, nodding.

"So… what… how… how does it work when a shifter claims a human woman?"

"They fall in love. They live happily ever after. Make babies."

"Do they… shift too?"

"You or the babies?"

"Either. Both."

"You, no. You will continue to be who and what you have always been. But the children would shift."

"Even if there were girls?"

"Again, it just doesn't happen much anymore. But if it did happen, yes."

"Okay," she said, looking away for a moment, letting all the information settle in. "Um, and, what about when you're, you know, a wolf? Would you, you know…"

"Force you to become interested in beastiality?" I supplied, chuckling. "No, baby. No. What we have in that way, we have in this form. The wolf is… different. More base and primal. Most interested in protecting you, being there for you, that kind of shit."

"Okay. Um, I have one more question. It's an important one," she clarified, but there was a light dancing around in her eyes.

"Shoot."

"When you… shift or change or whatever… do you always end up naked after? Because I think I might be into that," she told me as her gaze slipped down my naked body.

"Careful, baby. You're hurt. And I'm not that in control of those urges right now."

"I mean… it's just my ankle," she said, eyes getting heavy-lidded. "I'm sure we can think of ways to accommodate it. Besides, I hear orgasms are really good for pain management," she added.

There was no stopping the growl that moved through me, or my cock from going rock-hard in record time.

I didn't stop to think.

I didn't try to be a better man.

I practically fucking pounced on her, pressing her flat on the hard ground, my lips taking possession of hers, kissing her hard and deep, with all the pain and uncertainty we'd both been feeling since that first time on the front porch, when I'd finally made her mine, and she'd made me hers.

Sex, yeah, it was usually good.

But sex with your perfect person? Fuck, that was something else entirely.

Knowing what laid ahead of me, I lost all control.

My hand reached down under her shirt, grabbing her breast, twisting her nipple into a pained point, then sucking it into my mouth as she arched up off the ground, pressing deeper into my mouth, whimpering for more.

I wasted no time carefully removing her shoes so not to hurt her ankle anymore, then yanking off her pants and panties.

"Way, please," she whimpered as I sat back on my heels to watch as my thumb teased over her clit.

I could never deny her any-fucking-thing. Least of all this, that I wanted just as much as she did.

Grabbing her hips, I yanked her up onto my lap, then thrust inside her tight, wet heat, feeling her walls tighten around me, drawing me in deep.

"Fuck," I hissed as she moaned.

"Move, please," she begged, her hands grabbing my arms, holding on as I started to fuck her.

Hard.

Deep.

Reaching down, I grabbed her, pulling her against my chest, then getting to my feet with her, walking a few feet, then pressing her back against a tree, fucking her harder and faster, her moans filling my ears as her pussy got tighter and tighter as she got closer and closer.

"Come for me," I growled, feeling my own release coming.

Then, just like that, she was spasming around me, dragging me with her until we were both panting and spent.

"What's funny?" I asked a few minutes later as I felt her jiggling against me with her head buried in my shoulder.

"It's just… I think I've read this book," she said.

"What book?" I asked, looking down at her.

"Where a hapless girl gets banged by a supernatural creature in the woods."

"Been fantasizing about this for a while, huh?"

"You're better than the vampires," she told me.

"I fucking better be."

"Oh, my God. Are… do those exist too? And fairies? And demons?"

"If I tell you, are you going to start fantasizing about some horned demon?" I asked.

"Please. Like a horned demon can turn into a giant puppy and keep me warm all night."

"Puppy?" I grumbled, getting a giggle out of her.

"Big, scary, not puppy-like at all, wolf," she clarified.

"That's better. Come on, let's get you dressed and home, so I can wrap up that ankle of yours."

"I think I should give up on physical activity. I just seem to keep getting myself into trouble. Being mauled by wild animals, hurting my ankle…"

"Don't worry. I plan to keep you active enough to keep your cardiovascular health in check," I told her as I helped shimmy her pants back up her legs.

"Well, that is one kind of exercise I think I can get behind," she decided, taking her shoes from me, then letting me lift her up into my arms.

"I'm sure I could hobble. This is far," she objected after a minute or two.

"No."

"Come on. I know you're strong, but…"

"But nothing," I cut her off, having a feeling the conversation was going to turn to her getting down on herself. Which I wasn't about to allow. "I'm enjoying the fuck out of this. Don't ruin it by trying to say some untrue shit about yourself."

"Are you… bullying me into being nice to myself?" she asked, lips twitching.

"Hey, if it works," I said, smiling when she rested her head against my shoulder. "For the record, you're fucking perfect. And any second you spend thinking otherwise is a waste of precious fucking time."

"You just… did more for my self-esteem than an entire adolescence in therapy," she admitted as we closed in on the house. "So, if we are, you know…"

"True Mates," I supplied.

"Yeah, if we're that. Does that mean you are going to do all the manly tasks around here? Because I tried chopping wood again. And I'm reasonably sure there is a real threat that I might slice my own head open."

"Well, we can't be having that. And, yeah, I'm happy to keep you warm, baby. In all the ways I can do that. And we can be at the cabin, but we will also have to spend time with my pack."

"Your pack," she repeated, her gaze slipping away.

"Before you let your mind run away with you, they are going to love you."

"You can't possibly know that."

"I can. I do. You, Maribelle, mean a future for this pack. No one of my generation has met their True Mate yet. You will give all of them hope that they will find theirs eventually as well."

"What happens if they don't?"

"Then it seems like it will be up to the two of us to repopulate this area with wolf cubs."

"We should probably practice how to do that. You know… in case we are *forced* to do so."

"How many times a day do you think it would take to make sure we've mastered it?" I asked, already wanting to go another round. But I had a feeling that, with her, I was never going to *not* want her.

"Oh, three or four times at least," she declared.

Once I got her home and her ankle all wrapped up, we went for round two.

By the end of the day, we'd met her quota. And then some.

It was the fucking happiest I'd been in my entire damn life.

And it looked like I had a long future of similarly perfect days.

7

Maribelle

It was the full moon.

And Way had told me that I wasn't allowed to tag along while he went into the woods.

I'd been a little disappointed at first before I realized that, yeah, watching him hunt down sweet little woodland creatures might not exactly be good for us.

I understood that his wolf had impulses.

And that all meat meant harm to some animal somewhere.

But I just… I didn't want to be privy to that.

I guess it was true what they said about how in happy relationships, partners were allowed to have a little mystery to them.

So I didn't watch him hunt.

And he didn't watch me slather on a mud mask and a deep hair conditioner.

It was almost three in the morning when I heard a howl that had a smile immediately stretching across my face as I made sure I got all the mud off my face, then rushed across the cabin and out onto the front path.

Before I remembered what Way had said about enemy packs, brother turning against brother.

Because right there in my front lawn stood half a dozen massive wolves of all different colors, but each one of them sniffing, growling, and scratching at the ground.

My stomach tensed as everything inside of me screamed to run. But, yeah, I wasn't entirely sure that a pack of shifters who were, you know, part-human would be stopped by something as simple as a door.

So I did the only thing I felt I could do at that moment.

I screamed.

The sound made the wolves jolt back, clearly not expecting that reaction. But then their hackles raised as I reached for the only thing nearby. Which happened to be the damn broom I swept the front porch with.

And then, well, then the growling and snarling started, and I was confronted with half a dozen sets of extremely large teeth.

Panic was a hand around my throat, tightening with each passing moment, making my scream die as I ran out of breath.

But then, out of nowhere, there he was.

Leaping over the side of the front porch railing, and running in front of me in all his wolflike glory.

This was the first time, though, that I'd seen him angry.

Like the others, his hair was raised, his stance was tense, and a horrible snarl escaped him as he suddenly flew off the porch and at the closest wolf, taking him down on the ground where the two of them rolled around, growling, snipping at each other, but not seeming to do any actual damage.

Confused, my gaze slipped to the others gathered around, finding them all watching the display of the two wolves, but their hair had gone down, their stances had relaxed, and no one was snarling anymore.

I immediately looked back at wolf-Way, watching as he tussled with the other, lighter-colored wolf. Both were letting out yelps, but no one seemed bloody.

Were they, like, play fighting? Like dogs would do?

There was still so much I had to learn about wolves, about shifters, about how they interacted.

And since I had no intentions on ever giving up Way, I guess I had a lifetime with him to figure it all out.

Suddenly, walking down from the woods, I saw yet another wolf. This one darker than the rest. His coat was pure inky black, so dark that if I hadn't seen his eyes—a pure, ice blue—I would have missed him in the darkness.

The rest of the pack parted around him so he could get to the front, where he stopped to watch the scene of the fight before letting out a growl so ferocious that I jumped back and gripped my broom more tightly, holding it across my body like a shield.

Just like that, though, the two wolves sprang apart.

And just as quickly, they both shifted back into human form.

Not a second or two later, so did all the others.

"Oh." The sound kind of escaped me without thinking because, well, they were all stark freaking naked. Six or eight of them.

Balls-out naked.

And from my quick glance, all just as muscular and well-built as Way.

My head shot up to the sky, studying the blanket of stars as a blush crept across my cheeks.

"We're not shy, sweetheart," a smooth, clearly amused voice called.

"Mmhmm, that's great," I agreed, nodding, but still looking at the sky. "Good for you," I added. "I'm sure there's nothing to be, you know, shy about."

"Baby, it's okay, you can—" Way started.

"Baby?" a deep, gravel-like voice barked.

I didn't have to look to know it came from that black-coated wolf.

But my gaze shot in that direction anyway.

There he was.

A man so tall and strong and, well, scary, that he had to be their alpha.

Way was tall. By anyone's standards. But this guy towered over even him. He was well-muscled with pure black hair, a ridiculously chiseled face, bright blue eyes, and a scar down his jaw.

"Yeah, I have some shit we need to discuss," Way said, nodding.

"You've been missing for weeks. We had to track your scent out here," the alpha said. "And you just… have some shit to discuss."

"I told Garrick I was going away for a bit."

"You told Garrick a couple of days. It's been weeks with no word. You're not a fucking pup, Waylon. You know that shit doesn't fly. We thought you'd been taken by another pack when we found your tent and campsite empty. And when we tracked your scent here," he said, waving at the cabin. "Well…"

"She's my True Mate, Elden," Way said, shrugging.

"Your…" Elden said, glancing over at me, giving me a long look, then back at Way. "No shit?" he asked.

"No shit. I was in the woods one night and I felt it. Then there she was."

"And you didn't tell me, why?" Elden demanded.

"Because she's Greta's granddaughter," he said, and the entire pack stiffened, then looked over at me, making me want to shrink back into the house.

"Is she now?" Elden asked, jaw tight.

"And so I wanted to… get to know her first before I told the pack. Before I got everyone's hopes up."

"So that's what you've been doing? Getting to know her?"

"Yes."

"And what have you learned?"

"She's the one. And she wants to be the one. And her grandmother's business with our old alpha, that's their business and has nothing to do with us."

A growling noise moved through Elden at that, a sound I found impossible to analyze.

"Alright then," Elden said, nodding.

"Baby… now about you see if you can grab some towels for the pack?" Way asked, shooting me a smirk, knowing how uncomfortable I was with all the nudity.

I went ahead and rushed into the house.

Sure, I knew that if I was going to be around the pack a lot, I was probably going to need to get used to all the nudity. It was just, you know, shocking, is all. We lived in a very fully-clothed society. Nudity was almost always reserved for intimate partners.

I would adjust.

Until then, I would buy some extra towels since every one in the cabin save for the two in the hamper, were being handed out to Way's pack to wrap around their waists.

"Can I, ah, get you guys some coffee?" I asked, shifting on my feet under their intense inspection.

I suddenly understood why Way had decided to keep me secret for a while. I didn't know them well, but I could see the expectation and hope in their handsome faces.

They saw me as the future of the pack, and I couldn't help but feel a little, I don't know, judged. Even if that wasn't their intention.

"Tell you what," Way said, moving over to me. "How about you guys head back to the house. Catch a couple hours. And then I will bring Maribelle there later to meet everyone."

"Sounds like a plan," Elden said, nodding. "I'm Elden," he said, reaching a big hand out to me. "The alpha of the pack."

"Maribelle. It's nice to meet you," I said, trying not to shrink away from the penetrative way he was looking at me.

"You too," he said, finally letting my hand go, leaving me to open and close it to ease the sting as he and the others turned and walked toward the woods.

"You okay?" Way asked, his arm going around me, pulling me to his side.

"Yeah. That was, ah, intense. Especially Elden."

"That fuck has a gaze that can see right through you," he said, nodding.

"He really does."

"And you are everything he has always wanted since he knew he was the alpha of our pack. So he's looking especially hard at you."

"Oh, great," I grumbled.

"Not like that, baby. He's not judging you. I think it's more that he's... trying to understand what to look for. If that makes any sense. But he doesn't need to. He will know it when he feels it. I sure as hell did."

"Who was it that you were fighting with?"

"Garrick," Way answered. "My best friend."

"Right. I always pounce on and nip at my best friends too."

"It wasn't personal. I came in hot because you were screaming and scared, but as soon as I saw them, I knew. But he needed to learn a lesson for snarling at you."

"I shouldn't think that's as hot as I do," I admitted.

"Oh yeah?" he asked, his hands already going down to sink into my ass, dragging me up against him.

It wasn't long before we were both stark naked on the front porch and he was slamming inside of me from behind.

Hard.

Deep.

Soon enough, though, until he was grabbing me, turning me, and slamming me back against the house before surging inside of me again.

"You're so fucking beautiful," he growled, his hand framing my face, watching me as he drove me up to that edge, then sent me crashing down from it.

"Everything changes now, doesn't it?" I asked a while later as we made our way to bed, exhausted, needing a reset before we went to meet back up with his pack.

"What do you mean?" he asked, watching me with furrowed brows.

"We can't hide away here all the time anymore," I clarified, turning away from the bed and going toward the closet, wanting to grab something I'd been working on each time he went out for a run.

"We can be here as much as you want. But I think you will like hanging out with the guys. That wasn't the best introduction. They were worried and then… caught a little off-guard. They're a good time. And it is nice to have others to rely on. I know you're not used to that. But I think you will like it if you give it time. What do you have there?" he asked as I started to turn with it in my arms.

"Your quilt," I told him, giving him an unsure smile before spreading it out in front of me.

It wasn't anywhere near as good as my grandmother's quilts, but she'd had so many years of practice. I was just starting out. I had to keep reminding myself of that as I worked on it.

It was mostly green with some brown that made it look like the forest, like the trunks and leaves of the trees.

Then right there near the feet of the woods was a gray body of a wolf standing there, his head tilted up in a howl at the moon I'd placed further up by the corner.

"Baby…" he said, gaze slipping up from the blanket, a smile spreading across his face.

"I know it's a little rough. I have a lot to learn. But, I…"

"Nope. Stop. It's fucking perfect," he told me, coming closer, reaching for my face with both hands, and pulling me in for a kiss.

Long, deep.

Then we climbed in under the quilt in the cabin that I'd driven to like a last hope.

And what did I find?

Everything.

I found myself, my roots, my future, Way.

I found *everything*.

Things I hadn't even known I'd been searching for.

I wouldn't pretend to know what the future held. What I would do for work. What it would be like to get through the winter in the cabin, to start working the land in the spring, to connect with Way's pack and find my place within it.

But I did know that I had Way.

A connection deeper than soul-level.

I had a love that couldn't die.
Everything else, well, it would fall into place.

Epilogue

Waylon - 2 months

I knew the pack would be a bit intense at first, each of them having that marrow-deep urge to find their own, and wanting to know what was it about Maribelle that made her my True Mate.

The problem was, it wasn't that Maribelle had something about her intrinsically that made her mine. She was just… the right person. And she finally stumbled upon me.

I had faith that the others would find their mates. In due time. When it was right.

Until then, everyone seemed to be enjoying having her around, a little softness, someone who made soup when someone was under the weather, made them each a quilt for Christmas based on their favorite colors and interests.

"You know how fucking lucky you are, I hope," Elden said as we sat by the lake, watching Maribelle cuddled up next to a mid-afternoon fire under four blankets, scribbling at the notepad she'd been working endlessly on for several weeks.

Working on her own version of one of those spicy paranormal romances she liked to read. Because, "I have a lot of personal experience on the topic now."

She'd finally quit her job about a month before, knowing she wouldn't need to have her soul sucked endlessly because the pack worked as a collective. We pooled and separated the money. She had no more financial concerns.

Free to do anything she wanted to do, what did she do?

She read.

She wrote.

She made quilts.

She hung with the pack.

And she loved me.

Elden's gaze was intense as he looked at my woman.

As the alpha, I understood that his drive was probably even stronger than the rest of us. He needed his mate, his children, his legacy.

"I do," I agreed, watching Maribelle as something she wrote in her notebook made her giggle. "You'll find yours. I'm quite a bit older than you, remember," I added, clamping him on the shoulder as I got to my feet.

"Fuck, hope I don't have to be an old bastard before I find mine," he shot back as I was walking over toward my woman.

"Making me look good, I hope?" I asked, scooting in behind her.

"Oh, didn't you know? I'm writing about hot horned demons," she said, laughing when I tugged her hair.

"How's it going?"

"Amazing. I mean, I've always known I liked getting lost in books. I guess I just never realized I could enjoy writing them until I tried. Have I mentioned how glad I am that I came back here?" she asked, leaning into me, turning her face into my neck.

"Not in the past, say, hour or so."

"Well, I am so glad I came back here. Because I found not only myself and my passion for writing, but you, and our future."

"Never been so fucking thankful you came back, baby."

"I think it's been an hour or so since I told you I loved you too."

"Well, that can't stand."

"I love you," she said.

"I love you back," I told her, giving her body a squeeze as I pressed a kiss to her head. "For-fucking-ever," I added, reaching for the ring I'd picked up a week or so back once the special order came in, then slipping it onto her finger.

Then there it was.

A simple band with a moonstone in the center. Not traditional, but with meaning for us.

"Yes," she said, turning to look up at me. "A million times yes."

The Navesink Bank Henchmen MC
Reign
Cash
Wolf
Repo
Duke
Renny
Lazarus
Pagan
Cyrus
Edison
Reeve
Sugar
The Fall of V
Adler
Roderick
Virgin
Roan
Camden
West
Colson

Henchmen MC Next Gen
Niro
Malcolm
Fallon
Rowe
Cary
Valen

The Savages
Monster
Killer
Savior

Mallick Brothers
For A Good Time, Call
Shane
Ryan
Mark
Eli
Charlie & Helen: Back to the Beginning

Investigators
367 Days
14 Weeks
4 Months

Dark
Dark Mysteries
Dark Secrets
Dark Horse

Professionals
The Fixer
The Ghost

The Messenger
The General
The Babysitter
The Middle Man
The Negotiator
The Client
The Cleaner
The Executioner

Rivers Brothers
Lift You Up
Lock You Down
Pull You In

Grassi Family
The Woman at the Docks
The Women in the Scope
The Woman in the Wrong Place
The Woman from the Past

Golden Glades Henchmen MC
Huck
Che
McCoy
Remy

Shady Valley Henchmen MC
Judge
Crow

STANDALONES WITHIN NAVESINK BANK:
Vigilante
Grudge Match

NAVESINK BANK LEGACY SERIES:
The Rise of Ferryn
Counterfeit Love

<u>OTHER SERIES AND STANDALONES:</u>

Stars Landing
What The Heart Needs
What The Heart Wants
What The Heart Finds
What The Heart Knows
The Stars Landing Deviant
What The Heart Learns

Surrogate
The Sex Surrogate
Dr. Chase Hudson

The Green Series
Into the Green
Escape from the Green

Seven Sins MC

The Sacrifice
The Healer
The Thrall
The Demonslayer

Costa Family
The Woman in the Trunk
The Woman in the Back Room
The Woman with the Scar

DEBT
Dissent
Stuffed: A Thanksgiving Romance
Unwrapped
Peace, Love, & Macarons
A Navesink Bank Christmas
Don't Come
Fix It Up
N.Y.E.
faire l'amour
Revenge
There Better Be Pie
Ugly Sweater Weather
I Like Being Watched
Primal

Under the pen name JGALA:
The Heir Apparent

PRIMAL

Jessica Gadziala is a full-time writer, parrot enthusiast, and coffee drinker who has an unhealthy obsession with acquiring houseplants. She enjoys short rides to the book store, sad songs, and cold weather. She lives in New Jersey with her parrots, dogs, bunnies, and a whole flock of chickens and ducks.

She is very active on Goodreads, Facebook, as well as her personal groups on those sites. Join in. She's friendly.

9 7 9 8 8 4 8 7 8 0 7 3 4